CHANEL L. FAYE

Baby Be Mine

Contents

1

Chapter 1

Clicking on the email from her friend, Kanesha Green's heart sunk when she saw virtual pink balloons floating on her desktop computer before an invitation to Yolanda's baby shower popped up on the screen. A huge boulder took root in her heart, submerging it in a sea of bitterness, envy, and disappointment that filled her soul. This was the fourth baby shower invitation she had received this year. It seemed everyone she knew was either pregnant or a parent already. Every woman except her.

She squeezed her chestnut brown eyes with fingers, a deep sigh leaving her broad mouth. She hoped the released air would halt the sinking bitter pain in her chest. Next month, she was turning thirty-nine, the looming birthday a neon sign that her dreams of a family—a husband and children—were only that ... a dream. Five years into her singleness and non-voluntary celibacy was a sure sign that marriage and babies were not going to happen for her.

Glancing at the invitation again, Kanesha wondered how she

was going to survive smiling through the celebration. Though happy for her friend, the thought of pretending to be content with her singleness to her friends at the baby shower was unbearable. In her group of friends, she was the abnormal, single, childless one.

Her eyes gazed out of the large floor-to-ceiling window in her office at work that framed the magnificent dark blue Pacific Ocean and Golden Gate Bridge. Having this view of San Francisco was one of the perks of being the marketing manager for a large publishing company. Her manicured fingers lightly tapped her mouth as she took a deep breath. At least one area of her life had gone according to plan. She had her dream job, promoting authors who wrote novels people could lose themselves in for a few hours—leaving behind their humdrum lives for a moment to experience adventure, action, and love. Love. One thing that had eluded her, her whole life. She read the invitation again. A measure of pleasure rose in her when she read that it was a co-ed baby shower. That meant she could drag her best friend, Cody, to the dreaded event. Him being there would be the only thing making it tolerable. She knew he would bitch and moan the whole time, but he'd go because she'd asked him.

A knock sounded before Jessica peeked in, her blond hair falling across her shoulders and face before she brushed it behind her ear.

"Hey, Kanesha, do you have a minute? I want to discuss Tiffany's book covers. I don't think the new covers complement the marketing brand colors for the book series."

Kanesha closed the email, along with Yolanda's invitation, and smiled at Jessica, glad to have a distraction from of her negative thoughts. "Sure. Why don't you come in and we'll discuss it?"

Kanesha absently sipped her red wine, her finger toying with a black springy curl from the loose hair flowing down her back. She sat at the pale brown bar at a popular Japanese restaurant in the Russian Hill neighborhood, waiting for Cody, who was an hour late. She was used to Cody's tardiness, which had gotten worse when he became a prosecutor at the San Francisco District Attorney's office. She glanced at her watch, her Cody-patience-clock starting to wane.

She was about to pay her beverage bill when Cody's tall build rushed through the door. Looking at him as he talked to the host, Kanesha appreciated Cody's lean build in a dark gray suit with a white dress shirt. The suit perfected his sun-kissed skin and dark brown hair. Though they had been friends since their freshman year in college, Cody's tall, dark, and gorgeous looks still set her heart beating at a faster pace. She grinned and gave a small wave when Cody glanced at her and pointed his finger toward her at the bar to the host. Cody walked over with the restaurant's host, who guided them to a black oak table with pale blue chairs set for two.

Before she could even place her glass of wine on the table, Cody gently grabbed her hand, stilling its movement. She glimpsed up into his chocolate-brown eyes, her mouth turned up into a slight smile as she waited for the inevitable apology that would come from his mouth.

"I'm really sorry. A deposition went on longer than I intended and by the time I looked at my watch, I knew it was better to come and apologize face to face than through a text."

She took a sip of her wine, wondering if she should make him grovel even harder, but decided against it as she needed him to agree to go to the baby shower with her. She gives him a mischievous smile. "I know, Cody, you have a *very* important job. No need for apologies."

He leaned back into his chair, his eyes appraising her as they slightly narrowed. "Okay, what's going on? What do you want?"

Kanesha twirled the stem of her glass, delaying her answer. A waiter arrived, giving her a reprieve as they gave their order. They had been to this restaurant enough times to have memorized the menu. Watching the waiter walk away to place their order, Cody turned to her. "Spill."

"What?" She gave a nonchalant shrug, her fingers sliding down the stem of the wine glass. "I understand that you were held up. No biggie."

His eyes narrowed even further, as if trying to figure out what she was up to. "Pssh. I know you want something. If not, my ears would be bleeding from your lecture about time management."

She parted her lips to speak when the waiter arrived with their meal and drink orders. A glass of wine for her and a bottle of beer for Cody. The smell of soy sauce and spice wafted to her nose, making her mouth water. She hadn't had lunch, as her nerves were too tightly wound up from the invitation.

Kanesha had attended plenty of baby showers, but Yolanda's invitation made her anxious and fearful that her chance of being a mother could be running out. Yolanda was her childhood friend, and their lives had been in tandem until they'd veered off in different directions when Yolanda married, and now she was expecting her first child. Yolanda, who had given no thought to motherhood, was actually going to be a mother, something that Kanesha craved with all her being. She'd always thought that she'd be a mother by now, but now that she was staring forty straight in the face, still childless, her dream was slowly fading.

"Are you ever going to tell me what's up with you today?" Cody's words broke through her thoughts. The steam from the food dissipated as Kanesha brought her chopsticks close to her mouth and took a bite. The taste of soy sauce, pork, and seaweed created a flavorful combination in her mouth. A moan escaped her lips as she swallowed. This was why they frequented the restaurant so much. She glanced at Cody and caught a simmer of heat from his eyes before he looked down at his plate and sipped his beer. She gave a slight shake of her head. She must have misread the look in his eyes.

"Well?" he said.

"You remember Yolanda, right?"

He scoffed. Boy, did he ever. "You mean the chick who ended up in my bed when you guys crashed at my apartment after a night of partying?"

"Yeah, her. And she was drunk. She didn't know it was your bed."

A dark brown eyebrow lifted. He used his chopsticks to pick a piece of his gyoza. "Drunk, my ass. She still grabbed my junk when she was allegedly *drunk*."

One side of her mouth turned up as she picked at her ramen with her chopsticks. "Stop. You know it was a mistake. She thought she was in bed with her boyfriend."

"I've interviewed witnesses that were better liars than her. Anyway, what about her? She's married, right?"

"Right."

He mumbled, "Thank god," under his breath, but it was still loud enough for Kanesha to hear. She tilted her head and gave him a hard stare. "I received a baby shower invitation from her."

"Okay? Why has it got you acting strange?"

"Well..." She played with the napkin on the table. "It's a co-ed baby shower, so... can you come with me?"

He groaned, leaning back on the chair as he dropped a piece

of gyoza back onto his plate. "No, Kay. You know I hate those types of events."

"Celebrating babies and new life?"

"Standing around talking about babies isn't what I'd call fun."

"There will be other men there who wish they weren't, so you'll be in good company."

"No."

The corners of her mouth turned down. "Please? I need you."

2

Chapter 2

"*Please. I need you.*"

Cody inwardly groaned. Kanesha knew that when she used the word 'need', he couldn't say no to her. Her needing him was his kryptonite. He wanted to be the one that satisfied her needs. Her wants. It had been the case ever since they became friends in college. He'd always wanted more, but Kanesha had firmly put him in the friendzone, and so far, he hadn't been able to crack the wall she had put up.

He drank in her dark brown skin glowing underneath the restaurant's overhead lights, jet-black curls tumbling down her back. She was absolutely gorgeous.

"Alright. But I'm only staying for one hour."

"Two hours."

"An hour and a half."

She rolled her eyes, her shoulders relaxing. "You drive a hard bargain, but I'll take it. It's next week Saturday. No excuses."

He sighed, scratching the small scar above his right eyebrow. One day, he'd learn to say no to her. Or better yet, she'd be the one saying yes to *his* demands. *His* wants. *His* needs.

The first time he met her flashed through his mind. Her opening the dorm room wearing black tights and a gray college hoodie, curls tumbling down her back. She had captivated his attention ever since, and he didn't mind one bit.

3

Chapter 3

Cody and Kanesha pulled up to the curb in front of a two-story pale gray house in Presidio Heights with a front garden, bay widows, and a sloping roof with black timber. The dark gray door had a huge poster saying, 'We can bearly wait. Welcome to Yolanda's baby shower', with a bear floating on pink and gold balloons.

Cody rolled his eyes at the poster. "I've already started the clock," he said as Kanesha pressed the doorbell. A stiff smile settled on her face. She tugged on her French plaited ponytail.

"Stop it. You might end up enjoying yourself." She shifted the presents from one hand to another. She wasn't looking forward to the baby shower either. Though thrilled for her friend, she couldn't help but feel the pinching pain of jealousy in her chest.

Yolanda swung open the door, her protruding stomach covered by the colorful caftan dress she wore. Her midnight hair fell in waves over her shoulders. She radiated with an inner light that brightened her yellowish-brown skin.

"Kanesha! I'm so glad you are here." She clasped Kanesha's

shoulders and pulled her into a tight hug, her belly hitting Kanesha's flat stomach.

"Of course. I wouldn't have missed it." She moved away from Yolanda's perfume-scented embrace and smiled, hoping her smile appeared genuine.

"Yolanda," Cody greeted.

"Cody," she replied stiffly.

Since bedgate, animosity had lingered between them like a foul smell.

"Congratulations," Cody said, gesturing to her mid-section.

"Thank you. Damien and I are very happy." Her hands cradled her belly.

Cody smiled. "How far along are you?"

"Thirty-seven weeks. Not long now until our daughter gets here," Yolanda said, waddling back into the wide hardwood hallway painted a creamy color, with a white trim near the high ceiling.

They followed her into the living room with a view of the street from the white bay windows. The gas fireplace was decorated with brown, white, and gold balloons, different colored bears, and pink and white rompers that hung on the mantlepiece.

"You can place your presents here." Yolanda pointed a finger to a table overflowing with gifts.

Kanesha made space on the table and placed the gift bags next to the many other presents.

"Everyone is already at the back. I think you guys are the last to arrive." Yolanda waddled to the large eat-in kitchen with stained-glass windows and a glass sliding door that led to the garden.

The small area was packed with small children running around and friends of Yolanda and Damien. Music played from a stereo system. Damien manned the barbeque grill with a group of men holding beers and glasses filled with brown liquor.

Yolanda stroked her belly. "Why don't you guys make yourselves at home? You can grab some food and drinks. Cody, Damien can introduce you to some people."

Cody lifted his mouth in a one-sided smirk. "I know a dismissal when I hear one." He nodded and headed toward the men.

Yolanda turned to face Kanesha. Anger darkened her brown eyes. "You brought Cody? Really?"

"What? He's my best friend."

Yolanda's thinly shaped eyebrows shot up to her hairline.

"Uh, I mean after you, of course," Kanesha quickly amended.

Yolanda huffed, her belly moving with her breaths. "Cody is a nuisance and a distraction."

"A distraction?"

"Yes. A distraction from you meeting a man. Instead of finding a date for my baby shower, you brought him. How long has it been since you've been on a date? Better yet, had sex?"

Kanesha ran her fingers along her collarbone, her eyes focused on Cody—who had already made friends with the men and was laughing and having a beer.

"Cody's not the reason that I'm single."

"If he's always available to be your plus one, you'll never make an effort to put yourself out there and find a man. One day, Cody will get married, and where will you be then? A middle-aged single woman."

Anger bubbled inside Kanesha, warming up her body so much that the hot weather felt suffocating. She waved her hand to cool herself.

Yolanda looked at her with concern in her eyes. "I'm not trying to be mean. I just don't want to see you waste your life waiting for something that might never happen."

"What do you mean?"

"Something between you and Cody."

Shock reverberated through her. She closed her hands into fists to stop them from shaking. "You are out of line, Yolanda. Cody is *just* a friend. Next time, keep your unwanted opinions to yourself."

She stomped back into the kitchen, the air-conditioning cooling her heated body and her anger. Platters of food and a jug of iced water were on the marble kitchen counter. She poured herself a glass and sipped, leaning against the counter. Yolanda had gone too far, insinuating that she was waiting for Cody. Cody was her friend. A dear friend. That was all. But she had to admit that Yolanda was right about her depending on him for everything.

Although Cody wasn't the reason she was single, he made it easy to be. When she needed a date, whether for work events, weddings, or the dreaded baby showers, he was available, making it easy not to feel the emptiness of no romantic partner. And she enjoyed Cody's company. More than some men she had dated.

Cody got her sense of humor; she could be her true self around him and not put on a pretense. Cody knew all her pet peeves, her imperfections, her secrets, and he still wanted to be her friend. He was there when she needed help, advice, or to just sit quietly together. Sometimes, Cody knew her better than she knew herself. The thought of him settling down with someone had never crossed her mind, as his relationships never seemed to last long. The longest was six months, and that had been a long-distance relationship.

The marble counter was cool against her bare arms. She placed her elbows on the counter and covered her face with her palms. Why did the thought of Cody becoming serious with someone fill her with dread? This was Cody—good natured, funny, goofy, kind, annoying at the best of times, thoughtful Cody. Her *best friend.* There had been a time, when she had first got to know him and he had been dating her dorm roommate, during her first month as a freshman, when she'd thought she had a crush on him. Those feelings had been squashed when Cody became her friend, even after he had ended his one-month relationship with her roommate.

Of course she wanted him to be happy with someone. But that would leave her on her own. Single and childless. Completely alone.

"Hi Kanesha. Are you okay?"

She removed her face from her hands and glanced up. Ava, a friend from college, stood in the kitchen holding her six-month-old baby on her chest, the baby busy guzzling from a bottle.

"Yes. Just taking a breather from the heat."

"It is a scorcher of a day. I'm taking him up to change his diaper. I'll see you when I come down?"

"Yeah. He is a cutie, isn't he?" Kanesha said, trailing her hand down the baby's chubby hand to grab a tiny finger. She gazed into his blue eyes. A knowing bloomed inside of her, zapping her right in the stomach. This was what she wanted. She wanted to be a mother. She wanted a baby.

4

Chapter 4

Kanesha studied the photographs of smiling parents and children on the doctor's wall. Thank you cards littered the office, placed next to the doctor's certificates.

"Ms. Green."

"Kanesha."

The Indian doctor smiled, red lipstick bringing out the dark tone in her skin. "Kanesha, your scans and test came back all positive. Everything looks good. The anti-Mullerian hormone test shows good egg count at your age. There are a good number of follicles in your ovaries, and they are a good size. Your body is perfectly primed for conception. If your primary objective is to become pregnant soon, then I would suggest artificial insemination. It is cheaper and less intrusive than IVF. The question is, how ready are you?"

A wide grin broke out on Kanesha's face. She held in a squeal. "I've waited a long time for Mr. Right, and he isn't coming. I'm ready. I want a baby now."

"Good. You stop taking the pill and then we'll start you on a course of Clomid and Letrozole to stimulate your body to ovulate multiple eggs. We'll then schedule the artificial insemination. Now, all you have to do is go through the list of potential sperm donors, which we will email you, and choose your preference for the insemination."

Kanesha sighed, her shoulders moving with her breath. "Okay, Dr. Khatri. Thank you so much.

Dr. Khatri grinned, her white teeth brightening up her face. "Thank me when we get you pregnant."

* * *

Kanesha scrolled down the list of potential sperm donors. Their names were mere numbers, next to details such as age, occupation, and medical history. Was she really doing this? Making a baby with a faceless stranger? Her full lips pressed together in a grimace. It wasn't too different from meeting a stranger at a bar, having unprotected sex with them, and getting pregnant. At least this way, she knew it would be safer than unprotected sex. She wanted to be a mother, and this was how she would do it.

A knock sounded at her apartment door. Kanesha rose to open the door for Cody. He beamed, holding up a grocery bag. "Snacks and wine for movie night."

Grabbing the bag from him, she walked to the open-plan kitchen and started to unpack it. Cody removed his tie and unbuttoned the top two buttons of his dress shirt. "Ah, that feels good. Had a helluva day, and this tie felt like it was choking me."

"I saw the news. I'm sorry your trial ended in a mistrial."

Cody tilted his chin down and frowned. "Thanks. We are going to pursue the charges again in a new trial. We'll get him next time." He rounded the kitchen counter and stood next to the open laptop. "I know it's your night to choose a movie, but I'm really not in the mood for the sappy films you like to watch. So, I'm selecting one for us."

"Pssh. No, you're not. I'm not watching some green lizard men fighting in some galaxy far, far away. They look disgusting, and it's boring."

His eyes widened and his brows drew together. "I'll have you know, the Lizard Men of the Intergalactic is *the* greatest film ever to be made. I can't believe I'm friends with someone who doesn't get that."

Cody's eyes flicked downwards to the laptop, the screen still on the sperm donor list. "What's this?" He pulled the laptop closer and sat down on the kitchen stool, confusion clouding his face as he read.

Kanesha stopped looking for dishes for the snacks and quickly closed the laptop. "It's nothing."

Cody shook his head and raked his fingers through his hair. "Nothing? That looked like a list of sperm donors. Why are you looking at sperm donors? Is it research for a book you're promoting or something?" A questioning look flitted across his brown eyes.

Kanesha twirled her fingers before crossing her arms to stop fidgeting. "No, it's not research for a book. It's research for me to get pregnant."

"Pregnant?" he almost squeaked.

"Yes. I want to be a mother. So I'm thinking of insemination."

"What?" He grabbed the edge of the kitchen counter as if to steady himself.

"After Yolanda's baby shower, I made a decision to become a mother. I went to a fertility doctor and—"

"And now you're at the stage of choosing a sperm donor? When were you going to tell me any of this? I thought we told each other everything?"

Kanesha moved back slightly, giving herself space from Cody's questions. "I was going to tell you, but I was waiting for the right time."

"After Yolanda's shower would have been the right time. When you made the doctor's appointment—any time would have been the right time," Cody accused.

"I don't know why you are getting so angry. I'm just looking at my options."

He pointed at the laptop. "You're looking at sperm donors! It seems like your mind is made up. What about waiting for the right guy and having children that way?"

She wrapped her arms around herself in a loose hug. "I'm tired of waiting for the right guy. He doesn't seem to be coming anytime soon, and I'm afraid if I wait too long, I'll have missed my chance at being a mother. You know the biological clock is real. I'm turning thirty-nine, and no man in sight. This..." She pointed at the laptop. "Is within my control of getting what I want."

She opened the kitchen drawer and removed the wine opener, going to work with uncorking the wine Cody had brought.

He exhaled loudly. Pinching the bridge of his nose. "If you're serious about this—"

"I am."

He moved closer to her and stilled her hands. "Then I'll be your sperm donor."

Kanesha froze and stared at him, her chestnut eyes searching his for any hint of a joke. "What are you saying?"

"I'll be your sperm donor."

* * *

The shock reflected on Kanesha's face must have shown on his. Cody couldn't believe the words that left his mouth. He had never thought he wanted kids, yet the thought of Kanesha with a rounded belly from another man's seed filled him with jealousy. If she was going to be pregnant, then it would be his. No one else's.

He rubbed his neck. "I mean, why use a complete stranger's sperm? Why not use sperm"—he coughed—"from someone who cares for you?"

He looked at her as she pulled a kitchen stool and sat down. A myriad of emotions flowed through her. Confusion, disbelief, shock showed in her beautiful face.

She sucked in a quick breath, a stunned look on her face. "Are you serious right now? This is important to me. Don't play with my emotions."

Cody moved closer, placing a hand on her shoulder. His eyes focused on hers. "I'm dead serious. I want to do this with you. *For* you."

Her eyes watered and lone tear fell down her cheek. "Cody. I..."

She rose from the stool and pulled him in for a tight hug. Her eyes squeezed so tight that more tears flowed. "I don't know what to say. This will be the greatest gift ever." She moved away, breaking the hug, wiping the tears away. "Wow. I'll call the fertility clinic tomorrow to schedule an appointment for you to go and give a sperm donation."

"Whoa. I'm not masturbating into a small container."

Her body tensed, her shoulders slumping as she sat down on the kitchen stool. "I thought... You just said..."

He cupped her cheek and tilted her head until her eyes met his.

* * *

The golden rings that surrounded his pupils burned with lust, the heat scorching her insides as her body flooded with warmth. "If we do this, then we are doing it the natural way. No sterile container, no artificial insemination. That's my one condition."

Kanesha swallowed, her mouth feeling parched. "But we are friends. We can't sleep together..." Even when she said the words, her thighs pressed together, trying to stop the aching between them.

He cocked an eyebrow. "Haven't you heard of friends with benefits? The benefit this time will be a baby. *Our* baby." Leaning in, he brushed his lips against hers. The peck was light as a feather, but it ignited a flame in the pit of her stomach. She knew if she gave in, it would burn her alive.

Her full lips tasted sweet and luscious. He deepened the kiss like a thirsty man taking his first sip of cool, refreshing water after being dehydrated for a long time. Cody had wanted to kiss her for years. Since the first month of their freshman year. He had broken off his relationship with her roommate when he realized he only liked going to their room to see Kanesha. And now that he was having his taste of her, he vowed to never let her go. She was his and no one else's. He reluctantly broke off the kiss. "Is it a deal?"

She gazed at him with eyes hazy with desire. "It's a deal."

5

Chapter 5

Kanesha stared out of her office window, but instead of the Golden Gate Bridge and the endless blue ocean filling up her mind, the words "it's a deal" echoed through her head. Did she just agree to sleep with her best friend? The heat from his kiss had ignited parts of her that had laid dormant for years. Tingles had risen goosebumps all over her body when Cody's tongue had tangled with hers in a sensual dance. She had made the deal without a thought because she'd wanted more. More of Cody. More of what they could make. A baby.

A beep from her office phone indicating a call from her secretary brought her back to the present. "Yes, Colleen?"

"You have a call on line one from a Dr. Khatri's office."

Kanesha's teeth nipped her bottom lip with nervousness. "Thank you, Colleen. I'll take it."

Kanesha picked up the line from Dr. Khatri. "Hello, doctor."

Dr. Khatri's voice came through the phone. "Hello, Ms. Green. I'm just calling because my office informed me that you canceled

21

your appointment for this coming week. I thought we were on schedule to get you on the fertility drugs to get your body ready for insemination?"

"I know doctor, but I gave some thought on trying to get pregnant naturally first before... uh... the artificial insemination."

A pause permeated the air before Dr. Khatri spoke. "Oh. Then try to monitor your ovulation cycle and have sex as regularly as you can. If after six months there's no pregnancy, then we can try to add some fertility drugs to help facilitate a pregnancy."

"I will, doctor."

"I wish you well in your journey to motherhood," Dr. Khatri said before saying her goodbyes.

Kanesha took a deep breath and smiled. She was on her journey toward motherhood and with the best man she knew in her life. Her smile slipped, a fluttery feeling in her stomach. As much as she wanted to be a mother, she didn't want to destroy her friendship with Cody. Sleeping with him would change the course of their friendship. What direction would the friendship take? She had no idea. She just hoped it wouldn't be the end of it.

* * *

Cody couldn't stop the goofy grin on his face as he twirled his pen. He was supposed to be studying the criminal case before him, but his mind was on the fact that Kanesha had agreed to his harebrained idea of letting him father her child. It was an implosive decision, but he knew in his gut that it was the right move. Kanesha may think that it would be a short-term arrangement until she got pregnant, but she was wrong. Dead wrong. He wasn't letting her go. He was going to show her that he could be more than just a friend.

"Earth to Cody. Yo!"

A bundled-up wad of paper hit him square on his chest.

"Wake up, man," James said, standing on the opposite side of Cody's polished mahogany desk. "I've been standing here for a full minute. What are you day-dreaming about?"

"None of your damn business." He grinned, leaning back in his black ergonomic chair. He dropped his pen on the open file. "What do you want?"

James tilted his head to the side, his green eyes slowly examining Cody. "For a guy whose media-frenzy case ended in a mistrial, you are chirpy. Normally, you'd be studying the case again to see where you'd gone wrong."

James was right. Cody should have been deep into the detective notes, evidence, and law books to see how he could get a verdict in the retrial—while also litigating other criminal cases. Being a workaholic was how he buried his feelings and pretended that being Kanesha's friend was better than not having her in his life.

It was an excuse he'd used since college. Now, with Kanesha trying to get pregnant, it was a way he could show her that he could be more than a friend. More than a shoulder to cry on. That he was the man she had been waiting for. And he had been under her nose all this time.

"I'm working on other things in my life at the moment. Better things," Cody said, smiling, reclining even further in the chair.

He was working on making Kanesha his. And that was the most important work he'd ever do.

6

Chapter 6

Kanesha knocked her trembling hand on Cody's apartment door. She unclenched her fists and wiped the sweatiness on her yellow summer dress with little blue flowers and thin strips that showed off her toned shoulders and arms. The yellow color glowed brightly against her dark skin. If they were going to sleep together, she'd have to make Cody see her as a sensual being and not the frumpy freshman from college.

The door opened. Cody stood by the entrance dressed in dark blue jeans and a black t-shirt that showed off his lean, muscled chest. One of her shoulders rose, and her head tilted toward it as she admired him. Her heartbeat increased, and the tip of her tongue wetted her bottom lip.

"Hey, Kay, right on time. As usual," he jested as he stepped aside to let her in.

She chuckled softly. His lack of time keeping was a running joke between them. Her silky hair with soft curls brushed against her bare back. Kitten heels clacked on the hardwood floor as she strolled into the apartment hall that led to the living room. Her eyes widened as she took in the change of Cody's Marina District apartment. Gone were the sport and sci-fi memorabilia that used to decorate the living room and the worn-out sofas with food stains. Instead, the apartment had been redecorated with calming neutral tones that created an elegant design aesthetic. Black and white photographs of San Francisco lined the walls. A creamy white L-shaped sofa graced the living room, with a brown leather table ottoman. A huge plasma television was mounted on the wall facing the sofa.

"Wow! Cassandra did an amazing job on this place. It went from a frat house to a stylish apartment," she gushed, stroking the linen sofa.

He rubbed the palms of his hands together. "Cassandra was better at being an interior designer than a girlfriend."

Kanesha cocked an eyebrow, her hip angled against the sofa. "Did you break up with her before or after the renovations?"

"She broke up with me. She thought she'd move in after the apartment was done. She thought the relationship was more serious than it was."

Kanesha crossed her arms. "Maybe you gave her that impression." Her arms tightened around her. Is that what he'd do with the decision to have a baby with her? When it got too serious, would he bail? Though Cody had always been there for her as a friend, this was new territory for them. She didn't know if she'd be able to depend on him. Her heart pounded for fear that crossing the line into a sexual relationship might screw up their friendship. She shook her head slightly. Even if the worst happened with her and Cody's relationship, it would be worth it when she held her baby in her arms.

"I never promise things that I don't mean. It was all in

Cassandra's head, and when she realized she had gotten it all wrong, she left. And it was the right decision."

She bit her upper lip. "And you mean it? Having a baby with me?"

He stalked toward her like a lion closing in on its prey. "I promise that this is what I want. I'd do anything to give you what your heart desires."

Her heart flip-flopped like a salmon swimming upstream. His eyes blazed with an intensity she'd never seen in him before. Her body reacted with a flood of warmth that settled below her belly. Kanesha blinked before looking away from the fire that magnified the coppery tint in his eyes. If she gazed any longer, she'd burst into flames.

* * *

Cody trailed a finger across one of Kanesha's crossed arms. They were tightly wound around her like a comfort blanket. Touching her made his cock semi-hard. He wanted to taste her sweet, luscious lips again, but she looked like a skittish kitten ready to scurry away from his apartment. Cody knew she wanted to have a child—by any means necessary—but she still wasn't convinced she should be getting intimate with him.

A slight smile lifted the side of his mouth. Kanesha didn't know that when she'd agreed to his proposal, she had become his. Only his. And he would fight any man who would try to take what was his. He'd been patient all these years, but that wasn't enough anymore.

"I should put the steaks on the grill. We'll eat in the kitchen,"

Cody said, making his way to the newly designed kitchen with domed pendant lights hanging above the black and white granite-topped island, and black timber cabinets, creating a modern monochrome style of black, white, and gray tones.

Kanesha settled on the all-black swivel bar stool and feasted her eyes on Cody cooking and plating up their dinner. His lean muscles under the tight t-shirt flexed with every movement he made. He placed utensils and a glass of wine near her plate. "Bon Appetit," he said, grinning.

She returned his smile and picked up a knife and fork to slice the steak. A buttery and spicy smell wafted as she took a bite. Her eyes closed, savoring the juicy tender flavor. "Mmmm," she breathed out.

"You like that?" He smirked, the gentleness in his eyes meeting hers. She blinked rapidly, her tongue darting out to touch her lips as she squirmed in her seat. What was going on with her? When did she start feeling nervous around Cody? This was *Cody*, her laugh-out-loud friend.

"It's very good. But you've always been great at cooking, so..." She shrugged, tugging a loose strand of hair behind her ear.

"I'm great at other things too," he winked.

Was that sexual innuendo? Heat rose from her neck to the top of her head. Who was this new Cody? She took a mouthful of wine, stopping herself from using her hand to fan the blaze underneath her skin.

Cody scratched the back of his neck, stubble darkening his jaw. "Kay, we've known each other for twenty-odd years now. How come you've never mentioned how much you wanted children?"

"I've always thought that one day I'd have them." Her fork pushed around the sauteed vegetables on her plate. "When mom died and then dad followed a year later... being an only child, I-I feel alone. With my thirty-ninth birthday looming, I fear that my chance to be a mother is slowly closing and that my family's legacy will die with me. And that..." Her fingers rubbed between her collarbones. "It scares the hell out of me."

The clinking of the knife and fork hitting the near empty plate sounded as he released them and clasped her hand. "You'll never be alone. Not when I'm still breathing."

She gave his hand a light squeeze. "I know you mean it now, but someday you'll be serious about someone and start a life with them. And that life will come first. As it should. Then where will I be?"

"You'll..." He pressed his lips together before taking a sip of his wine. "That won't happen."

* * *

Didn't she know that she *always* came first with him? That was the reason why his relationships with other women never lasted long. They were never her. When she called, he came running, and it constantly caused problems in his relationships.

"That will never happen," he stated. He twirled the wine glass, the stem fragile in his hand.

She lifted an eyebrow, not quite believing him. "At least if we make a baby together, we'll always have that bond between us."

He cleared his throat. "Talking about making a baby, when should we start?" He held his breath. *Please say now. Please say now.*

A shy smile curved her mouth. "The doctor recommended having sex regularly. So, I guess anytime is a go."

Cody gently clasped his hand with hers, his thumb stroking

the soft inside of her palm, tracing her life line with it.

"I want you to know that I've never had unprotected sex with anyone. My last doctor's check was last month, and I'm clean." He smiled, a wicked glint in his eyes. "Can't wait to go bareback with you."

* * *

The stroking of his thumb and his words had her squirming on her stool. Heat traveled from her hand to settle in a swirling motion of desire in her stomach. Her face flushed and she took a sip of her wine.

"I'm clean too," she said.

He pulled her up with the hand he held and led her to the front of the kitchen counter. His hand dropped to her waist and drew her closer to him. Her breasts brushed against his hard chest, sharpening the pool of desire within her. She thought she had buried the feelings she had toward Cody during freshman year, but they were rising up inside her. Slowing spiraling. Tilting her head, her eyes focused on his mouth. She desperately wanted him to kiss her.

He answered her need, crushing his mouth against hers in a hot, intense meeting of tongues, teeth, and lips. She knew her mouth would be swollen from the bruising kiss. He gently nipped her lower lip with his teeth before pulling away from her.

"We'll never get to dessert if we keep this up," he said, his voice low and tinted with longing.

She giggled. Was she really going to have sex with Cody? Feel his lean masculine body move on top of her? Her body temperature notched up to a full-fledged hotness. Wetness soaked her panties.

"I think dessert can wait," she breathed out before capturing his mouth with hers.

He pressed her against him, his hand moving down to her lushly rounded buttocks, pulling her even closer, wanting her to feel the need and desire for her in his groin. Cody shuffled backward toward his bedroom, making sure not to break the kiss. If there was any break in the kiss, it might give her pause and she might change her mind—not about having a baby—but about him.

They stumbled into his bedroom. Their hands touching and stroking all over their bodies. His t-shirt fell to the carpeted floor, and the thin straps of her dress fell down her shoulders, revealing the swells of her breasts.

Cody's bedroom was dimly lit by one lamp, casting shadows over his dark brown furniture and king-sized bed. The small light gave Cody ample view of Kanesha's breasts rapidly rising and falling with her breaths. He kneaded her ass cheeks, relishing their softness in his hands. The dress was getting in the way. He wanted to feel her silky skin. He scooted back, breaking the kiss, pulling the dress over her head.

Her wavy hair cascaded down her bare back. His breath caught in his lungs. Standing there, nearly naked except for her bra and panties, her mouth swollen from his kiss, and her dark skin glowing in the dim light, Kanesha looked like a fallen angel sent to tempt and torment him. She stood before him, her body graceful with shapely hips and slender legs. He swallowed; his mouth dry from the lust that consumed him.

She looked better than in his dreams. Dreams he'd had since college. Now here she was, panting slowly, and he couldn't wait any longer to make his dreams reality. His hands, which shook slightly, went to her back to unclasp her bra. Her boobs gently bounced when freed from the lacy material. Cody trailed kisses on the slope of her throat, breathing in her scent of soap and a floral mixture of jasmine and rose. The ache in his groin increased, his dick straining against his jeans, wanting to be released and claim what was his. He took deep breaths. He needed to calm down or he'd come in his pants like a virgin teenager. Turning slowly as he licked and kissed the hollow in her throat, he gently placed her on the firm bed before moving back to hastily remove his jeans and boxers.

Kanesha smiled at the sight of Cody clawing at his pants and roughly pulling them down, nearly tripping on the legs of his jeans. Straightening, he gazed at her with eyes that burnt with hunger and desire. A thrill went down her spine, making her shiver at the intensity in his eyes. This was a new side of Cody she had never seen before. Wicked and manly. His body was athletic, with broad shoulders, muscled thighs, and indentations in his abs that tightened with his breaths.

Her fingers tingled. She wanted to touch him. Feel the firmness of his skin, the sprinkling of his chest hair, and... She gazed down to his long, veiny, thick, glistening dick that jutted out, stiff against his taut stomach. Warmth flooded her body, her eyes wide. Who knew that Cody was packing? Her mouth became moist with saliva. Her core clenched empty air, yearning to be filled by his manhood.

A devilish grin crossed his face as if he could read her mind. She slid up the bed on her elbows in jerky movements as Cody stalked toward her like a predator ready to capture its prey. He leaned over her, covering her body with his. Her breasts rose when she filled her lungs with air, brushing against Cody's chest, the friction causing her rosy-brown nipples to harden from her arousal.

He fused his mouth to hers in an earth-scorching kiss that made her toes curl. Her back arched at her need to be closer to him. To feel his warm, hard body against hers. Her heart thumped wildly in her chest, and she wondered if he could hear it. He broke the kiss, trailing kisses down her throat, moving down to her heaving breasts. She gasped as his wet tongue licked her nipple, his hand caressing the other. She felt longing, hunger, and an emotion she couldn't name. She was doing it, making a baby with her best friend.

Cody gently nipped her nipple before licking it and sucking it into his mouth. She tasted salty and sweet, a flavor that made his cock ache with need. He turned to the other breast, giving it as much attention as he had the other one.

"Kay, you taste so good. So good my l—" He was going to say his love. It was too soon to voice such emotions. It would scare her and stop this. He didn't want it to stop. He needed her too much. Instead, he let his hands and kisses show his love for her. His hand glided down her toned stomach and slid into her lacy underwear. He traced the thin strip of hair that led to her slit. His heart skipped a beat as he felt how ready she was for him.

"Oh baby, you are so wet," he said, his voice hoarse with lust.

She moaned and writhed beneath him as he placed two fingers inside her hot, tight sheath and thrusted, coating them with her wetness.

"Mmmm," she moaned.

He removed the two fingers and tugged down the panties until they slid down to the floor. He was getting impatient. He wanted to be inside her. Feel her tightness around his cock. Capturing her mouth with his, he nudged her thighs apart and settled between her legs, his dick straining and jerking at the thought of entering her.

He gazed in her heavy lidded eyes, glazed with lustfulness. Her eyes connected with his. His heart paused for a beat from how beautiful she looked with her hairline damp and her skin flushed from passion. Passion that he had caused. Cody's chest felt like it might explode with joy. His fingers laced with hers as he nudged the tip of his cock into her hot, wet entrance.

"O-ooh," he groaned.

Kanesha felt so good. Better than anything he could imagine. It felt like coming home. His body tightened from the tensity of trying not to burst inside her before she reached her climax. With one thrust of his hips, he slid inside her. She whimpered and moaned, her inner walls clenching around his hard, straining dick. His teeth clenched together, and a nerve jumped in his jaw as he fought against the tingling at the base of his back. Gaining control again, he thrust deeper, moving in a rhythm that was as old as time. Her hips pressed up to meet his thrusts, her slickness coating his cock with each move.

"Yes, Cody. Just like that," she said huskily, her sharp fingernails raking down his back. He was sure they were going to leave red marks. Marks he would wear proudly.

Kanesha's moans and groans grew louder, her breathing increasing.

"Yes, oh yes," she said breathlessly.

His tempo increased as he pounded into her, beads of sweat sliding down the groove of his back.

"Come, baby. Come for me," he coaxed hoarsely.

She squeezed her eyes tightly shut, her body arching off the bed, her lips parting as she gave a low, guttural moan. Her inner walls clenched when she reached her peak, squeezing his cock. He moaned from the sensation, and pleasure erupted inside him. He gave one deep thrust before giving up his control and surrendering to his release, sperm spurting out of his cock into her womb. It felt so good not having latex containing his cum. A shudder went through him at the thought that a baby could come from this encounter.

Cody tenderly kissed her damp neck, her cheek, and then finally her parted lips. Her heart rate thumped in her chest, her breathing slowly returning to normal. He rolled off her, taking her with him until half of her body lay on top of him.

He lay in bed, holding her against him. His breath took in the smell of their mating. A salty, musty scent that made him semi-hard even though he had just orgasmed. Cody gazed at Kanesha. Her eyes were closed and a light snore come from her.

Placing small pecks on her face, he brushed her hair away from her face. He stared lovingly at her peaceful face, the words "I love you" on the tip of his tongue. But he held them in. It wasn't the right time. She needed to be awake and alert to hear his confession of love. Tightening his hold on her, he closed his eyes and drifted off to sleep.

7

Chapter 7

Kanesha blinked as she rubbed sleep from her eyes. Her mind took a minute to register where she was. She was in Cody's bedroom, the morning light muted by the closed curtains. She felt a warm body underneath her, and she realized she had slept on top of Cody, who had his arm slung over her. As she shifted, his arm tightened around her, not wanting to let go. Sighing, she laid her hand on his chest, tilting her head back so she could watch him sleep.

Last night had been mind-blowing. Cody had conducted her body like the concertmaster at the orchestra, his touches and kisses tweaking her sexual tunes until she sang like a canary. He had made love to her—love, not sex—not like a man satisfying his urges or helping a friend have a baby. But as a man loving his woman.

Her heart tugged at that thought. His woman. She felt the yearning she had pushed down deep inside. She thought he'd never see her as girlfriend material, so had settled on being his friend because it was the only way to have him in her life. But the infatuation had come flooding back, even deeper and more real than in freshman year. How was she going to bury her feelings now? When she knew his touch, his kisses, and the feeling of him deep inside her. Her chest tightened and tears gathered. She was royally screwed. She gently moved his arm away and scooted away from him to start dressing to leave. She needed to get out of his apartment before she made a fool of herself.

"Where are you going?" Cody's sleep-laced voice asked.

"I was going home. To give you space."

"Kay, were you going to leave here like I was some one-night stand?" He wrapped his arm around her waist and pulled her close. "I thought you were on a mission to get pregnant, and the doctor said regular sex, right? So I'm sure morning sex is part of 'regular'." He wiggled his brows and grinned.

His boyish grin ignited a flame in her stomach, and she pressed her thighs together. They were sticky from her juices and his semen. They had forgotten to wipe themselves before sleeping.

She grimaced. "I think I need a shower, and then I'll go home to get dressed. I need to go to work." She sat up and slid to the edge of the bed.

His hand on her back halted her escape. Tingles flew down her spine as his hand traced the shape of her spine.

"You're going to work? It's Saturday. We normally go to brunch at our favorite café. I thought we'd have coffee here and then walk to the café."

She bit her lower lip. She desperately wanted to lay down and bury herself under his warmth, but she needed to keep the lines clear. This was only to have a baby. Nothing more.

"We have a big book promotion coming up this week. I have to finalize the details."

Cody's hand fell away, leaving her bereft. "Okay, I'll put the coffee machine on while you're in the shower."

She nodded, afraid her voice would betray her and show how much she needed him. Wanted him.

Gathering up enough nerves, she placed her feet on the carpet and stood, covering herself with her dress that pooled on the floor.

* * *

The water from the rainfall showerhead sprayed on her hand as she tested the temperature. Kanesha secured her hair into a messy bun atop her head to stop it from getting wet and stepped into the walk-in shower with black glazed porcelain tiles. She tilted her head up, the water sliding down her neck and front. She closed her eyes, enjoying the heat of the water. The hairs on the back of her neck stood up, sensing a presence behind her. She swiveled her head and saw Cody stark naked.

"Um ..." she said, baffled.

A salacious grin curved his mouth, the thin lines around his eyes deepening. "I thought we'd conserve water and shower together." He advanced toward her. The pupils in his chocolate eyes dilated with desire.

"I didn't know you cared so much about water conservation?" she said breathlessly, his body so near she could feel the heat radiating from it. He stepped under the showerhead, water pouring down his head. Cody edged away and slicked back his wet hair. Her heart pounded in her chest, her breaths coming out in short pants. Cody looked roguish with his hair darkened by the water, the morning stubble giving him a powerful virile energy.

"California is going through a drought, don't you know?" he quipped. Leaning forward to kiss her, he nearly toppled over as she quickly scooted away to press against the polished black subway tiles of the shower wall.

"Don't get my hair wet," she threatened.

Throwing his head back, he gave a belly laugh. "Believe me, I know all about black women's hair. You've explained it enough times. I won't dare get it wet. Now. Get. Over. Here."

He pulled her close, his back to the showerhead, shielding her from the pulsing water. He tugged a stray curl behind her ear, his touch sending tingles down her body. Cody squeezed some shower gel into a loofah and lathered up the space between her breasts before moving to soap up her breast, taking painstaking time with it. She gasped, her nipple a pebbled dark nub, each stroke of his hand sending jolts of electricity down to her pussy, which was dripping with need. He moved to the other breast and paid the same amount of attention to it.

Her knees buckled and he wrapped his arm around her waist to keep her from falling to the tiles. Positioning her against the wall, near the showerhead, he continued to clean her with the loofah, taking his time with her stomach, buttocks, and then her thighs. Closing her eyes, she breathed in the scent of black pepper, ginger, and lemon from the shower gel that permeated the glass-paneled shower. His touch sent shivers of excitement down her body, and she pressed herself against the cool tiles as if to escape the intense emotions raging inside her.

"Look at me," he commanded.

She opened her eyes. Stared into his. Dark with lust, affection, and a yearning that pierced her heart. Wobbling on her feet, she used the wall tiles for support as want and need gnawed in her aching core.

Cody dropped the loofah and positioned her under the showerhead—careful not to get her hair wet—to rinse off the residue of soap. When she was clean, he placed her back against the wall and dropped to his knees, kissing her belly before licking her belly button. She arched her body toward him as if to say, more, more.

A wicked grin crossed his face as he kissed and nibbled down her belly to her mound. Lifting one thigh, he balanced her leg on his shoulder and placed a hand on her stomach to steady her. She gasped and squirmed when his tongue licked her wet folds. He deepened the kiss, his tongue sliding inside her entrance. Her short, sharp breaths sounded loud in the shower. She gripped his hair and lifted her hips. He gazed up, his eyes aflame with passion. He licked his lips, wet with her slickness.

He growled. "You taste so good. So good. I could eat you all day."

Kanesha moaned at his words, her hips lifting, urging him to continue.

Cody held her wet core to his mouth. Her pussy clenched even before he took a long lick of her slick folds, a growl of satisfaction rumbling out of him. His tongue was everywhere. Lapping, licking, sucking, and gently nibbling, driving her to the height of carnal pleasure. He focused on her clit, circling his tongue before sucking. The powerful sensations from his actions made Kanesha twitch and wriggle under him, her head hitting the tile wall. Her eyes tightly closed as she lost her mind to the intense pressure rolling through her body.

"Open your eyes, Kay," he said huskily. "I want you to look at me. To see me."

She opened her chestnut eyes, darkened by lust. Confusion

broke through her muddled mind, heavy with desire. What did he mean? See him eating her like he was a starving man having his first meal in months? The visual drove the all-consuming bliss to new heights. Her panting breaths amplified, tension building inside her like a bomb about to explode.

"Cody, I-I can't..." she cried out. "I'm so close. Oh god, yes."

"Yes, baby," he said in between sucking her sensitive clit.

He increased the sucking, making her toes curl. Her pussy fluttered with the beginning of an orgasm, her chest heaving as she tried to get the moist air into her lungs. Kanesha's cries turned guttural as her body and mind catapulted into mind-numbing rapture. A sweet, pulsing thrill making her body shudder and break apart. Her cries died out; her mouth open in a silent scream.

Cody lapped up her juices, a sound of appreciation emanating from him.

As she came down from her sexual high, Cody stood from his kneeling position and switched off the showerhead. She had forgotten that water had been raining down on them.

"I need to be inside you," he rasped.

He lifted her and carried her bridal-style out of the walk-in shower, taking a towel off the hanger by the bathroom door as he strolled to his king-sized bed.

Gently placing her feet on the carpet, he patted her dry with the cotton towel before roughly wiping the droplets of water off his body. Dropping the towel on the carpet, he said, "Get on the bed, Kay."

His commanding voice sent excited shivers down her back as she scrambled onto the bed. He crawled over her gorgeous body. Pushing her thighs apart, he settled at the apex of her legs. Cody gazed at her with tenderness that tugged at her heartstrings.

His hand cupped her cheek, his thumb softly stroking it. He drove into her wet entrance and started an erotic rhythm that quickened her heart and made her cry out in ecstasy. He followed quickly after with a grunt, his hot seed filling her.

They lay pressed together in exhaustion, breathing heavily, contentment flowing through them.

Kanesha gave him a light punch on his chest. "Now I'll have to shower again."

He chuckled as he pulled her close, nuzzling her neck. "Oh, Kay. My Kay," he breathed out before falling asleep.

8

Chapter 8

Carina belted out a popular pop song, her cherry hair fiery from the red strobe light in the private karaoke room reserved by her friends and co-workers for her thirty-ninth birthday.

Kanesha poured champagne and politely smiled at the well-wishing from those close to her.

The day she was dreading was here and putting on a happy face was making her jaw hurt. She stretched her neck and took a sip of the champagne. The white synthetic leather of her bodycon mini dress stuck to her thighs.

"Alright, alright, alright. I think it's my turn," Cody said, stepping up to the stage and choosing a song to sing. Sounds of guitars and drums started, and Cody did an air guitar movement, while jumping in the air. Kanesha laughed. He looked ridiculous doing exaggerated air guitar in his work suit. He had removed his suit jacket and tie as the night progressed.

Singing the first lines of the song, he looked at her and winked. Kanesha recognized the song was The 1975's *Me & You Together*. It was one of Cody's favorite songs that he played repeatedly.

She pretended to be a fan girl, hollering and fluttering her lashes at him, making him hoot with laughter.

"Cody still making a fool of himself, huh?" Yolanda said from behind her.

Kanesha pivoted to see Yolanda and Damien with their arms around each other. Yolanda's loose dress still showed a rounded stomach though she had recently given birth to their daughter.

"You guys came? I'm so glad," Kanesha said, giving them hugs.

"Of course, we wouldn't miss your birthday. Though we can't stay long. My parents are babysitting Zuri. And if I'm away from her for too long, I start leaking like a faucet," Yolanda said, grimacing.

"Aw, I'll have to come see your daughter soon," Kanesha said, turning back to the stage to watch Cody, who stared at her with an intense hungry expression.

"Oh my gosh, you guys are fucking," Yolanda whispered in her ear.

Kanesha swiveled her head toward Yolanda. "What! No. We are not."

Yolanda gave her the I'm-no-fool look, arching one perfectly shaped eyebrow. "That's a look of a man who's seen you naked and would like to ravish you again."

A flush crept up her cheeks, the heat enhanced by the flickering strobe lights in the room. She pulled Yolanda away from Damien toward a quiet space at the back of the room.

"I've known you since eighth grade, Kay. You can't lie to me," Yolanda said, crossing her arms, her legs spread apart in a don't-mess-with-me manner.

"It's complicated, okay?"

Yolanda gave an un-lady-like snort. "Yes, it is complicated.

You are sleeping with a guy you've been in love with since college?"

Kanesha gasped, pushing her hair back from her face. "I'm not in love with Cody."

Yolanda's stance softened, her eyes flicking from Kanesha to Cody, who had finished his song and was strolling to the mini-bar area to get a drink. "You may be able to lie to yourself, but never to me. You're in love with him. And sleeping with him—when you know his relationships never last longer than a month—will hurt you, Kay. I don't want to see you hurt."

Kanesha gritted her teeth. "If you knew I was in love with him, as you put it, why did you try sleeping with him?"

"What?"

"That night you ended up in his bed."

The tiny muscles under Yolanda's eye quivered. "I was drunk and didn't know it was his bed," she seethed.

Kanesha held her hands up. "I'm sorry. That was out of line. It's just that you don't understand what's going on."

"Then explain it to me."

"I'm trying to have a baby, okay. Cody is helping me get pregnant. It's an agreement. Nothing more."

Yolanda's mouth fell open, her eyes bulging, and a wheezing noise come from her throat. "What? Pregnant? Are you crazy!" Her voice had risen enough to make their friends turn their heads to them.

"Shh, you're making a scene," Kanesha admonished.

"Don't shush me. For an intelligent girl, you are being very stupid right now. Have you thought about what will happen when the baby comes? Will you be together? Will you be parents together?" Yolanda blew out an exasperated breath. "Have you even given much thought to this?"

Taking a step toward Yolanda, Kanesha glared at her. "Yolanda, you're not my mother. I already had one, remember? I don't need another."

Yolanda held her hands up. "Fine. Do you, boo. But when it comes crashing down, don't come to me." She twisted away from Kanesha and headed to her husband. She whispered in his ear, making him turn his head to Kanesha, before they weaved their way through the groups of people and left the room.

Watching them leave, Kanesha's chest felt tight. She rubbed her hand over it.

"That looked heated. What was that about?" Cody said as he approached.

Staring at the stage, watching one of her friends dance to an '80s song, unable to look at Cody, she whispered close to his ear. "She knows about us."

"What? You told her?" Cody asked.

"No. She guessed. And I ended up telling her about our agreement." She peered at him. His eyes narrowed.

"I'm guessing she wasn't very supportive."

Her shoulders drooped. She sighed, trying to let out the stress bubbling under her skin. "No. She thinks it's a bad idea that we haven't thought through, and I think she may be right."

Cody's jaw muscle throbbed. "She doesn't know what she's talking about. We know why we are doing this. You becoming a mom. Right?"

She rotated her shoulders, trying to loosen the tension in them. "Right."

But she wasn't so sure anymore that she'd made the right choice by not going the sperm donor route. It would have been much simpler. She wouldn't have fought with Yolanda and, most importantly, she wouldn't be sleeping with her best friend, putting their friendship in danger of irreparable damage. When she got pregnant and Cody moved on, she knew she wouldn't be able to carry on just being his friend.

"Come here," Cody said, pulling her into a bear hug. "It'll be okay. You'll see." He placed a chaste kiss on her forehead, his eyes throwing daggers at the satin wall draping.

* * *

Fuck! Yolanda was such a bitch. Cody couldn't believe she'd stick her nose where it wasn't needed or wanted. His hands itched to pick up his phone and give her an earful, but he knew he'd just be giving her ammunition. He had wanted to end the night with Kanesha screaming out his name in ecstasy, but that plan had clearly gone to shit. Thanks to Yolanda.

"Come on. I think a shot is waiting for you, birthday girl," Cody said, leading her toward the bar, where some of her friends had congregated.

9

Chapter 9

Cody rapped loudly on Kanesha's apartment door. She stood in the doorway dressed in a black silk robe with delicate red detailing, the robe slightly open near the dip of her breasts. Her black hair hung over her shoulders in long coiled curls as she stared at him with confusion in her chestnut eyes.

"What are you doing here, Cody?"

He stood there for a second, his eyes taking in the alluring sight she presented in the mid-thigh robe.

She tilted her head to the side and pursed her plump lips. "Well?"

His eyes zoomed back to the peek of the bare breasts and his lips parted. "Um." He swallowed, his mouth feeling dry. "It's Friday. Our movie night."

Holding up the grocery bag with snacks and wine, he smiled. She let out an exasperated sigh and stepped aside for him to walk in.

"I messaged you to cancel," she said in a bad temper, closing the door with a loud thud.

Cody's eyes flicked around the familiar apartment. The walls of the living room were painted a pale purple color. Miniature Ghanian statues—bought during a student exchange program abroad—decorated the living room alongside bookshelves packed with books that overflowed across her living room floor.

"We never cancel movie night. And you've been avoiding me since your birthday. I don't know why you're allowing Yolanda to mess with your head." He placed the grocery bag on the kitchen counter.

Her brows pulled together as she crossed her arms, the movement edging up her ample breasts. How was a man supposed to concentrate with such temptation before him? Looking away, he focused on one of the wooden statues of a man posing in deep thought, a despondent feeling coming from the depiction. Cody knew the sentiment. He didn't know how he would convince Kanesha to keep to the agreement if she decided to end it. He needed more time to show her that they belonged together.

"Allowing her? She made good points, and I need to think," she said, stomping to the open plan kitchen. Opening the fridge, she took out a bottle of water, uncapped the bottle, and drank.

"Need to think about what? If you still want a baby?"

"No! I still want that. I need to decide if we should keep sleeping together. I could always go back to using a sperm donor."

He lunged forward, stopping a mere fraction from her. His eyes narrowing to slits, his nostrils flaring, he hissed, "I'll be your baby's father. No one else. Especially not some frozen sperm of a stranger. Do you understand?"

She placed the palms of her hands on his firm chest, which

rose and fell rapidly, and pushed him hard. He hardly moved an inch. "Don't talk to me like you are trying to control me," she seethed.

Grabbing her shoulders with both hands, his heart pounded in his chest. He gazed at her face, frustration and hunger darkening his eyes. "I'm not. I just need you to know that I want you to be mine. Do you get that?"

He crashed his lips to hers. Lifting her up, she wrapped her legs around his waist. Carrying her to the couch, he sat with her straddling him. Cody's hands explored her body as Kanesha fumbled with the silk tie of her robe. She slid the material off her shoulders with ease, revealing the breasts that were tempting him.

With his cock throbbing beneath her, he emitted a pleased grunt as she began to move her hips, his jeans and her thin, flimsy panties the only thing separating their bodies.

"I need you, Cody," she groaned.

"I know, baby. I need you too." Swiftly, he unbuckled his belt, unbuttoned and unzipped his jeans. Moving slightly, he pushed down his jeans and boxers, releasing his stiff dick. Moving her panties to the side, he lined his cock up with her entrance. Kanesha was already wet from grinding her body into his. With a satisfying sigh, she slid down his cock until she was seated to the hilt.

"C-Cody," she stuttered before slamming her lips into his. Her mouth tasted sweet and delicious. He devoured her mouth with deep, sweeping strokes of his tongue, kissing her like he needed her lips in order to breath. To live. He couldn't get enough of her.

"Fuck, Kay," he panted into her mouth as he tightened his grip on her hips, helping her with her pacing as his hips pressed forward to meet her thrust for thrust. Their eyes met in a soul-stirring look, filling his heart like a balloon ready to burst. They moved together as one, her breasts bouncing with their motions. He leaned forward and sucked one taut nipple.

Her breath quickened, sweat making her dark skin glow. He reached down where they joined and used his thumb to finger her clit. She groaned, arching her back, making it easy for him to lick and suck her erect nipples. Her body tensed, a wrenching cry breaking out of her mouth before she murmured his name over and over again. Her juices slicked his cock as her inner walls clenched on his throbbing dick, milking his climax from him. His jaw clamped down as his cock spurted hot cum into her welcoming womb.

He cupped her face and gently kissed her. She slumped down on his chest, her breathing slowly returning to normal.

* * *

Shifting onto the couch, she bent down to retrieve her robe and slipped it on. Her underwear, soaked from her juices and his cum, were sticking to her skin. Wiggling, she rolled her underwear down to the floor. Snatching them up, she held them tightly in her grip. She looked at Cody, who had his eyes closed, a tiny smile on the edge of his mouth.

"We can't keep having sex without talking about what Yolanda said," Kanesha said, awkwardly picking on a loose thread on her robe.

Cody swayed his head toward her, his satisfied expression gradually replaced by mild irritation. "And what exactly did she say?"

Letting go of the loose thread, she rubbed the back of her neck. "She made a point that we haven't talked about what will happen when the baby is born. And she's right. I was so ecstatic at the thought of being a mom, we just jumped straight into bed instead of discussing terms and conditions."

One dark brown eyebrow lifted. "Terms and conditions? Are we in a boardroom right now?" He pulled up his boxers and jeans, zipping them up.

She punched his arm.

"Ouch!" He exaggerated rubbing his arm.

"I'm serious."

He clasped his hand with hers. "So am I. I want to have a baby with you. Raise it together. I made a promise that I'm not going anywhere. And I meant it." He held up a three-finger salute. "Scout's honor."

"B-but what if..." She cleared her throat. "W-what if you meet someone? What will they feel about you having a baby with me? If I was the woman, I don't think I'd be comfortable with us hanging out together. Maybe she'll want you to keep a distance from us."

"That won't happen."

"How do you know? You—"

"It won't happen. Because there won't be another woman."

Her lips parted in bafflement. "There won't be another woman?"

Cody gazed at her with yearning, opening his mouth to speak when his phone rang on the kitchen counter. "Fuck," he muttered as he rose to answer it.

"Sullivan," he barked down the phone. Kanesha winced, feeling sorry for whoever he was talking to. He glanced at her while on the phone, his face growing frustrated at whatever he was hearing.

"Okay. Give me an hour. I'll be there," he said, before ending the call. "A state witness for one of my cases got shanked in prison. I have to go to the hospital and talk to the warden."

His long legs quickly covered the few paces to the couch. Tilting her head toward his, he gave her a scorching, claiming kiss. Breaking the kiss, he gazed into her eyes. "We're going to make a baby together, okay? And the rest... We'll figure it out."

Her mind still muddled from the kiss, she nodded.

Cody gave her one last peck before strolling out of her apartment.

10

Chapter 10

Kanesha woke up feeling tired and rundown. She had been tossing and turning these past two weeks, uneasy with the way Cody and she had left things the day he had dashed out of her apartment. They hadn't really resolved anything in regard to what would happen when she became pregnant. And what did he mean there won't be another woman?

"Kanesha? Are you listening?" Tayler's voice broke through Kanesha's fatigued haze. Heat burnt around her earlobes. How embarrassing to be caught daydreaming during a meeting with one of the publisher's bestselling authors. She blinked her sleep-heavy lids. Even after having had two huge cups of strong coffee, she still wanted to crawl into bed and sleep for a month.

"I'm sorry, Tayler." Kanesha smiled sheepishly. "As you can see from these mock-ups, these are the marketing materials that we will use for point-of-sale displays and your website, and we believe we can carry them to your social media campaign for your new release."

Tayler's baby blue eyes scanned her face, concern in them. "You look tired. Are you okay?"

Forcing a smile on her face, Kanesha nodded. "So, what do you think?" She pushed the printed pages toward Tayler.

Staring at them, Tayler smiled. "I love them. Your team did a great job as always."

Kanesha's smile was genuine this time. "Thank you. Don't tell anyone, but you're my favorite client." She winked conspiratorially.

Tayler chuckled as she rose from the soft padded office chair. Kanesha stood to give her a goodbye handshake when the world went black.

* * *

When Kanesha opened her eyes, she was in a hospital. She blinked in surprise, wondering how she had got here. The last thing she remembered was her meeting with Tayler.

"Oh good, you're awake," a well-built man with auburn hair in light blue scrubs said. "I'm Nurse Spencer. You were brought in after collapsing at your place of work."

"How long have I've been here?" Kanesha asked.

"Thirty minutes since the paramedics bought you in. The doctor ordered some blood tests and for me to take down your medical history."

Nurse Spencer rattled off some questions while writing down the answers. After the questioning was over, he drew some blood from her arm.

"Rest. The doctor will be with you shortly," Nurse Spencer said, a gentle smile curving his handsome face.

Kanesha laid her head on the flat hospital pillow and passed out again.

"Ms. Green?" a deep male voice called.

She opened her eyes, rubbing sleep from them. A bald man with a neatly trimmed beard stood over her, holding her chart.

"Our apologies for keeping you here for so long, but we've been waiting for your blood test results." He perused her chart. "I'm Dr. Wolowitz. You fainted due to low blood pressure caused by your pregnancy."

Gasping, her hand flew to her chest. "Pregnant?" she squeaked.

Dr. Wolowitz's brows furrowed. "I'm sorry. You didn't know." He looked down at her chart. "You are approximately three weeks pregnant. I'll recommend that you see your OB-GYN for further tests. For now, I suggest you take plenty of fluids and rest. The nurse will give you the release forms to sign and you'll be free to leave. Should we call anyone to come and get you?"

Swiveling her head, she asked, "Where's my bag?"

"All your belongings are in the bedside table."

"Then I'll call someone. Thank you."

Dr. Wolowitz gave a short nod. "Take care, Ms. Green."

He left to attend to another patient, leaving Kanesha reeling.

Pregnant? She was pregnant? Excitement, joy, and anxiety all fought for her attention. This was her dream. But she hadn't expected to become pregnant so soon. Her heart leaped into her throat. Cody had said he wanted this. But what about them? What would happen to their friendship now that a baby was a reality? Her muscles ached, and she felt that she could sleep for months. Worrying about her friendship with Cody was making her head hurt.

She took her phone out of her bag and found Cody's number. The call went to voicemail. A heavy sigh sounded out of her parted lips. She left a message asking him to call her as she was at the hospital and ended the call. After Kanesha signed the release forms, she requested a car through a ride-share app and went home to crash.

11

Chapter 11

Loud pounding and a male's voice calling her name woke her from a deep sleep. Her phone flashed with an incoming call. Kanesha had put her phone on silent before crashing.

Picking up the phone, she saw that the call was from Cody. Groggy from sleep, she rose from the bed, realizing that she had fallen asleep on top of the bedding, still dressed in the mossy green dress she'd worn for work.

"Kanesha! If you are in there, please open the door," Cody bellowed.

"Hey man, keep it down," a neighbor complained.

"Kanesha!" Cody called, ignoring the neighbor.

Staggering to the door, Kanesha placed a hand on her grumbling stomach, reminded that she hadn't eaten all day. Now that she knew she was pregnant, she had to take better care of herself. "Alright, I'm coming. Hold your horses, Cody."

She opened the door just as Cody raised his hand to pound again on her walnut veneer door.

"Cody! You are disturbing my neighbors," Kanesha chided.

He stomped right past her into her apartment, pacing in the space between the kitchen and the living room. "I've been calling and calling you, but you didn't answer your phone. The hospital told me you had discharged yourself, and you won't answering your door!" His face was blotchy with anger as he raked his fingers through his brunette hair. "You called me. Why didn't you wait for me?"

Kanesha took a step back from the anger radiating from him. "I did call and got your voicemail. I left you a message..." Her voice faltered. "But I guess I should have sent you a message saying that I went home. I'm sorry. My mind's been foggy lately."

Striding toward her, he placed his hands on her shoulders, sliding them down to her hands and holding them. "Are you okay? Why were you at the hospital?" Concern darkened his chocolate eyes.

Biting her bottom lip, she glanced down, studying the grout joint on the tiles. "I fainted at work, and they must have called the paramedics. I woke up at the hospital."

Cupping her face, he lifted her chin so her eyes met his. "Is something wrong? Are you sick?"

"No! Nothing like that—" She grimaced as her stomach took that moment to let out a big rumble. "That's embarrassing," she said sheepishly, "I haven't eaten since morning."

"How about we get you some food and then you tell me what's going on. Pizza be alright?"

She grinned and nodded enthusiastically.

"The usual?" he asked.

"Yep."

Cody phoned the local pizzeria and placed an order. Kanesha

went to her room and changed into baggy sweat shorts with a tank top. Her hair in a messy bun, she padded to the living room, where Cody slouched on the couch with his suit jacket lying next to him, a tie stuffed in its pocket. Cody's eyes scanned the length of her body, the heat in his stare dilating his pupils. The tip of her tongue licked her lips. A sharp intake of breath sounded from his mouth. He scratched the stubble on his jaw.

"Sorry I've been MIA this past week. When you called, I was in court getting a postponement on the case for the stabbed witness. He survived. Thank God. He is in protective custody. This whole week, I've been trying to find witnesses at the prison, but no luck. The prison guards all deny being there when he was shanked, and the prisoners want a deal before they say anything." He sighed. "It's been a fucked-up week. And then hearing your voicemail…" He gazed at her. "I got scared. I shouldn't have shouted at you."

She sat down next to him. Leaning in, he settled his head in the crook of her neck and inhaled her scent, his body visibly relaxing against hers. "I've missed you," he said.

Her heart leaped and lodged itself in her throat. He missed his friend. That was all. "We've gone without talking before. I'm used to it."

"No. I've missed being inside you. Kissing you. Holding you." He wrapped his arms around her trembling body. Cody pressed gentle kisses on her earlobe and down her neck and flickered his tongue on the dip between her collarbones. She gasped, her skin prickling with goosebumps, her pulse quickening with her breaths. Just when his hand found its way under her tank top, a knock sounded on the door.

Sighing with exaggeration, he stood up from the couch. "Such perfect timing," he said.

Kanesha laughed as Cody adjusted himself before heading to the door. He paid the delivery man and returned holding a large pizza. Her mouth watered as the smell of it wafted to her nose.

Biting into the pepperoni slice and swallowing it, her stomach revolted. The sensation of nausea overwhelmed her, and she ran to the bathroom, making it just in time to purge the small amount of pizza she had eaten. After emptying her stomach, she brushed her teeth and opened the bathroom door. Cody stood by the door holding an uncapped bottle of water. She grabbed the bottle and gulped down the cool, refreshing liquid.

"What's wrong? You really are sick. Do you want to go to bed?" he fired off questions, following her to the living room. She pressed her hand on her face, dragging it downward, wiping the clamminess of her skin.

"Cody." Placing the empty bottle on the coffee table, she put her hands up, palms facing forward. "I know what's wrong. The doctor told me at the hospital."

His jaw tensed and he clenched his arms to his chest. "Is it serious?"

Sidling up to him, she touched his arm. "It's serious. But I'm not dying. I'm pregnant."

His face beamed. Hoisting her up in his arms, he twirled them both, whooping loudly. "Pregnant! You're pregnant. Yes!"

"Cody! Put me down! If you don't stop twirling, I'm going to hurl all over your head."

Abruptly stopping, he placed her down. "Is that better?"

"Much better. Thanks."

Moving to the kitchen, he pulled open kitchen cabinets and then closed them.

"Um, Cody? What are you looking for?"

"Bread. My mother made us dry toast when we had an upset

stomach or vomited our guts out. It helped."

She cocked her hip and placed a hand on it. "Maybe you could try the bread bin?"

He turned to her, confused. "Bread bin?"

Pointing at the red steel roll top bread bin, she smirked. "That."

He smiled embarrassedly, his cheeks tinting pink. "Oh."

While he busied himself with making toast, he kept shooting her contemplative looks.

"What?" she finally asked.

"Are you happy? With the baby I mean."

Sitting on the couch, she breathed in and out, trying to sort out her thoughts. She was ecstatic about the baby. It was what she wanted. A child to love and nurture, a chance to see them grow into an amazing person. But now that she was pregnant, it meant the end of whatever this was with Cody. And she desperately didn't want it to end. She thought she would have more time with him.

"I'm happy. Excited even. But I thought, due to my age, it would take months for me to get pregnant. I guess I'm still shocked by it all."

He brought the two pieces of toast to her. She looked at them and scrunched her nose. "I have to eat those?"

"Yes. You haven't eaten all day and you just threw up whatever *was* in your stomach. You're growing another human inside you now, and you have to take care of them *and* yourself. How far along are you?"

"Three weeks. I need to make an appointment with an OB-GYN."

"I want to be there. For the appointment."

Her eyebrows lifted. "But you are busy. You don't have to

come."

"I'll make time." Crouching down, he placed a hand on her stomach. "The baby's part of me, too."

She scooted away, making his hand fall from her stomach onto her lap. "Cody. This is what I was talking about a week ago. When we decided that you'd be the sperm donor, we didn't come up with rules for how this will work."

His head tilted to the side, the hand on her lap curling into a fist. "How it will work is that I'm this baby's father, and I'll be there for every appointment and anything that comes up."

She squeezed her eyes shut and opened them again. Playing happy families with Cody, when it was all an act, would kill her. Instead of enjoying her pregnancy, she'd be miserable. "What if I don't want you to?" she said, her voice small. "I was willing to do this alone, and I still want that."

Eyes flashing with anger, he stood up. "No, Kay. You are not going to do this. I know this all started with you wanting a sperm donor, but I know you felt something between us. And this thing. This love. We made a life, and I'll be damned if I'm not part of it. If I'm not *part* of your life. I'm your best friend! Your lover. I'm not going anywhere."

She leapt to her feet, her index finger poking his chest. "Yes. You are my best friend, and I don't want to lose that ever. Sleeping with you will just make everything complicated, and I'm afraid that it'll mean the end of our friendship. And I'll protect that with all my being. That will mean stopping us from sleeping together and playing happy families."

He leaned forward so her finger pressed hard against his chest. "You seem to have forgotten what I said to you last week. You are mine. There won't be anyone else. Not for me. You will *never* lose me." The golden rings around his pupils glowed intensely.

"You've always had me. Since the day we met in college. All you had to do was see me. But all you saw was a friend, so that's what I was. Hoping that one day, just one day, I'd have my moment to show that I could be more than a friend. And now that I've had you, Kay, I'm *not* letting go. Especially now that you are carrying our child."

He moved to hold her, but she scooted away, shaking her head repeatedly. Her heart was beating so fast, she thought it would pop out of her chest. If he touched her, she knew that she would cave. Because she wanted to be in the safety of his arms, his warmth, to heat the coldness that seemed to have invaded her skin. But she was afraid that when the sexual haze had evaporated and he was stuck with a baby and her, he would leave. Cody had never had a serious relationship last for more than a month. When he inevitably left, he would carve out her heart and leave with it. And there'd be nothing left for her and the baby. She had to protect them both.

Cody stepped closer to try to hold her again, but she held her hands up, palms facing forward to stop him.

"I can't do this," she choked out.

Brushing his nose several times with his index finger, his nostrils flaring, a loud sigh escaped his mouth. "Can't do what? Let me love you? Let us be a family? What can't you do?" he said, stressing each question.

"Can't you see that I'm doing this to save our friendship?" she argued.

"Fuck our friendship! I've spent years pretending that I didn't love you. Didn't lust for you. Burn for you. That I was content with being a friend. But I can't do that anymore. It hurts too much. So fuck our friendship. We can have so much more, but only if you let us."

She stood there, biting her lip, unsure of what to say. She wanted to throw caution to the wind. But fear gripped her heart so tight that she stood trembling before him.

Cody gritted his teeth, his muscles tight as he waited for her to say something. Anything that would indicate that she wanted to be with him as badly as he wanted her. The longer she stood there not speaking, the more dread filled his body. All these years, he had assumed correctly. Kanesha had only seen him as a friend. Even now, carrying his child, she couldn't see him as a romantic partner. She couldn't see that the man she had been waiting for all these years had always been right in front of her.

His head felt heavy, and he ran his hands over his face. "Okay. I won't push you anymore. You've made your choice. I'll be there for the baby. Every doctor's appointment, the birth, and for the rest of his or her life. But you and I being friends... I can't do that anymore. Call me with the date and time of the first appointment." He stared at her for one more moment, searing her with his look filled with anger, longing, and anguish before stalking out of her apartment.

With the sound of the door banging shut, Kanesha dropped to the floor, tears falling down her face. She thought she was doing this so she wouldn't be alone. And now the one person she had always relied on had walked out of her life. Lying on the cold tiles, she covered her face with her hands and sobbed.

12

Chapter 12

Though Yolanda had been adamant that Kanesha shouldn't contact her when everything went up in flames with Cody, Kanesha had to reach out. She had no one else to talk to, and she needed someone to help her sort out her conflicting thoughts and emotions these past few weeks.

The moment Kanesha said "Hello", Yolanda knew something was wrong. She agreed to meet for lunch the next day. Yolanda had been hurt when Kanesha started sleeping with Cody and didn't tell her. She thought they talked about everything. But hearing the pain in her friend's voice, she knew she had to put her pride aside and be there for Kanesha, even if it meant giving her some tough love.

They met in the Mission District in an open-air rooftop restaurant that overlooked the busy mission street and the Bay. Kanesha arrived, waving at Yolanda sitting in one of the high wooden tables with black cocktail chairs.

"My gosh, girl. You look rough," Yolanda said.

Kanesha's mouth narrowed as she sat. She hated the high

cocktail chairs. They were too uncomfortable in her tired state. Plus, Yolanda wasn't wrong in stating how awful she looked. Her eyes were puffy, and she had dark circles from lack of sleep and crying.

Yolanda's expression softened. She covered Kanesha's hand with hers. "What's going on? I'm guessing it has to do with Cody?"

Annoyed with herself, she wiped the tears that started to gather. When was she going to stop crying? *Bloody hormones.*

"I'm pregnant," Kanesha murmured.

Yolanda reeled back in surprise. "Pregnant! Congratulations! Why do you look miserable though? Isn't it what you wanted?"

"It was. I mean, it is. I do want the baby. And I'm so happy about that. B-But Cody ended our friendship. Anytime I see him, he's so cold towards me. I've never seen him act like that before with me. A-a-and I don't know how to fix it. I miss him."

Yolanda tsked. "I told you that Cody is feckless and commitment phobic. He ran away when it got real, right? Can't handle that he'll be a dad?"

Memories of Cody getting teary-eyed when they heard the baby's heartbeat for the first time at the doctor's office made her clench her hand into a fist.

"Yolanda, can you please stop Cody-hating for just one day and listen to me?" she berated.

Yolanda waved her hand as if swatting a fly, her mouth twisting to the side, but she said nothing.

"Thank you," Kanesha said, gazing at the view. "The night I told Cody I was pregnant; he declared his love for me. Said he's always wanted me since college."

Eyes widening, Yolanda's jaw hit the floor. "What? Since college?"

Kanesha nodded.

"Well, he hid it well. So, what's the matter? You've wanted him for just as long. Didn't you get together and become one big, happy family?"

Giving Yolanda a pointed look, Kanesha scowled. "You may be wrong about many things regarding Cody, but you are right about him being commitment phobic. And I'm afraid that when the whole newness of us being a family fades, he might one day just realize that it's not for him and leave. And I won't survive that. It's better that we stay friends. Then he'll always be there."

Cocking her head, Yolanda lifted one eyebrow. "I'm confused. He's in love with you. You've always been in love with him. Why are you so hung up on being his friend?"

A tear ran down Kanesha's cheek. "I don't want to lose him. And us becoming more than friends will *guarantee* that will happen. You and he are the only family I have, and I can't lose any more family. My parents were foster children with no parents and grandparents. I was their only child. Now with them gone, I don't want to be alone in the world."

"Oh, honey." Yolanda held both of Kanesha's hands in hers. "I remember Mrs. Green always saying you were her miracle child," she said, grinning as Kanesha's mouth lifted into a small smile. "When your mother died, and a year later your father, you had the rug pulled out from under you. Since then, you've let fear rule your life. Any type of change scares you, and you cling to what is familiar. Cody's relationship with you changing must be terrifying. But you can't let fear stop you from happiness and possibly the love of your life."

A nervous laugh broke through Kanesha's lips. "You think Cody might be the love of my life?"

A thoughtful expression crossed Yolanda's face. "I know I've always maintained that I don't remember going to Cody's bed that night. But I lied because I was embarrassed. Cody had been going through girls like a newborn goes through diapers." She smirked. "Anyway, I assumed he'd note the invitation and sleep with me, but instead he reacted like a bug had crawled into his bed. He took his pillow and went to sleep on the couch. But I guess now I know that he didn't sleep with me because he knew it would have meant that you and him would never happen."

Leaning back, Kanesha crossed her arms. Her eyes narrowed. "You tried to sleep with Cody even though you knew I had a crush on him?"

"I thought, seeing what a playboy he was, you'd stop liking him and date someone you had a chance with. I didn't know he liked you as well. See, if you are angry with me for something that happened with Cody years ago then you really have it bad. Just go tell the guy you love him too and get both of you out of your misery." She held out a menu. "Can we order now? I'm starving."

They laughed and called a server to their table.

In the middle of the night, Kanesha went to the bathroom. When she pulled down her panties, they were covered with blood. The world began to spin. With shaky hands, she dropped the ruined panties in the bathroom bin and went to find fresh ones with a pantyliner. Her body covered in a cold sweat, she called Cody. Pacing her bedroom, she prayed he would answer her call.

A sleepy hello came through the phone receiver. "Cody! I'm bleeding. Something must be wrong. Please can you come get me and take me to the hospital?"

She could hear the springing of a bed, opening and closing of drawers. "I'll be there soon. Don't panic. It's going to be okay," he reassured her.

Getting dressed in pants and t-shirt, she waited for Cody in the living room, her hand on her stomach, talking to her baby, asking her to stay safe and alive. She knew deep in her gut that the baby was a girl, and she prayed that she'd get to hold her one day.

A knock sounded on her door, and she scampered towards it. She opened it to find a rumpled Cody, wearing sweatpants and a t-shirt. A far cry from the suited prosecutor he embodied each day.

"Are you ready?"

She gave a curt nod.

"Then let's go."

She grabbed the apartment keys by the door and clasped the hand he held out.

* * *

Cody drew in a deep breath as the car stopped by the hospital's automatic sliding doors. Hoisting her into his arms, he carried her to the Emergency Department. A female nurse rushed towards them. "Can I help you, sir?"

"Yes. She's pregnant and bleeding. We don't know what's wrong."

"How far along is she?"

"Um, nine weeks, nearly ten," he answered.

The blonde nurse looked at Kanesha. "Ma'am, we'll take you to the OB-GYN department. They'll assist you there."

They placed her in a wheelchair and wheeled her to the elevators. Cody followed closely, his hand on her shoulder. The look of terror on her face made his chest tighten. He wished he could do something, but he was out of his depth. If this was a court room, he'd know what to do to save his baby and the woman who held his heart.

When they reached the department, the nurses in pink scrubs helped Kanesha into a room and a bed. The pungent smell of ammonia, antiseptic, and artificial cleaner assaulted his nose as he took deep breaths to steady his heart. He stood by the window that overlooked the parking area of the hospital. His fingers drummed against his thigh. Closing his eyes, he prayed to any higher power that their baby was still alive.

"The doctor will be with you soon," a brunette nurse said to Kanesha. She turned and smiled at Cody before leaving the room.

"Cody." Kanesha sniffled, wiping her nose with the back of her hand. "Please tell me it's going to be okay."

He closed the few spaces between them and wrapped his arms around her. Her head rested on his chest. He wished he could say it would be okay, but he had never lied to Kanesha and he wouldn't start now. Instead, he held her close, hoping his presence gave her comfort.

A dark-skinned woman in navy blue scrubs strolled in followed by a nurse. "Hello, Ms. Green, I'm Dr. Walters," she said as she looked at the chart. "You came in with bleeding while nine weeks pregnant?"

Kanesha nodded, her eyes watery and puffy.

The doctor gave Kanesha a reassuring smile. "Now, we are going to check what is going on. Please place your legs on the leg rests."

Kanesha scooted down and placed her legs in the stirrups.

"I'm going to do an ultrasound to check your baby's heartbeat and your cervix to see where the bleeding is coming from.

Okay?"

Kanesha stared at Cody before nodding. Dr. Walters looked at Cody. "Do you want him to leave the room?" Dr. Walters asked.

"Oh. No. I want him here. He's the baby's father."

Cody gave her a look that told her he would have put up a fight if she had asked him to leave.

After the examination, the doctor pulled up a chair and sat near Kanesha. Sitting up, Kanesha's lips and chin trembled. The doctor placed her hand on Kanesha's arm. "The news I'm sure you are waiting to hear is that your baby is fine. The fetal heartbeat is strong."

An audible sigh of relief sounded in the room from both Cody and Kanesha.

Dr. Walters grinned, showing straight white teeth. "Your bleeding was caused by a subchorionic hematoma, which is a common complication during the first trimester. We hope the bleeding will stop by itself and not get any heavier. I would recommend that you do a follow up appointment with your regular OB-GYN. When you guys are ready, you can go home and monitor the bleeding there. I advise you to avoid strenuous activity, heavy lifting, or excessive exercise. And you need frequent rest to prevent any increase to your blood pressure. The nurse will help with the discharge papers."

The doctor stood. "I have to do my rounds now. I wish you all the best in your pregnancy." She smiled and left the room.

13

Chapter 13

Kanesha's sleep was deep and dreamless. She drifted awake with her hand snuggled around her stomach, cradling it. Her heart twisted in pain. She thought she had lost her baby. Spreading her hand out on her stomach, she whispered, "Hang in there, little one. Mommy can't wait to meet you."

Sounds of pots and pans banging in the kitchen made her head jerk up in surprise. Cody must still be here. He had gone to sleep on the couch last night instead of driving back to his apartment. The feeling of ease and comfort that had always been there when she knew Cody was around was replaced by nerves and a tingling feeling in the pit of her stomach.

She swung her legs out of bed and strode to the en-suite bathroom. She splashed warm water on her face and made herself presentable before taking timid steps toward the kitchen. This was ridiculous. This was Cody. Her best friend for almost twenty years. Instead, she felt like a junior in college again with a massive crush on her friend, all warm and buzzing with electricity.

She had buried her feelings for Cody because she thought it was best for their friendship, but Cody's declaration of love had created a chasm in their relationship. No matter what, it was never going to be the same.

Cody turned to look at her as she stepped into the open kitchen, his brown eyes taking in her yoga pants and t-shirt.

"Did you sleep alright?" he said as he whisked pancake batter. "Hope you are hungry; I'm making your favorite buttermilk pancakes."

Her stomach rumbled at the thought of fluffy pancakes with maple syrup and melting butter. "Mmmm. Can't wait. I'm starving, actually."

He nodded toward a kitchen stool. "Have a seat. It'll be a minute."

Continuing to study her as she sat, he placed the bowl of batter down and checked the heat of the skillet. The sounds of Cody pouring batter and flipping pancakes filled the kitchen. Yolanda's voice swelled in her mind. Was she letting fear stop her from love and happiness? Her increased heart rate pounded in her ears, her mouth dry from nerves. She couldn't let fear dictate her relationship with Cody. She loved him more than a friend, and after all these years, he'd admitted that he felt the same too. So what was stopping her?

She licked her dry lips, swallowing the lump in her throat. It was time to push down fear and embrace courage and love. It was right within her grasp. The family she'd always wanted after she had lost her parents.

"Cody?" she said, her voice rising in pitch. She felt the heat of a blush on her cheeks.

"Yeah?" he said absentmindedly as he placed the brown

pancakes on a heated plate.

"I love you. And I want to be with you."

His head whipped around, shock and surprise in his widened eyes before tenderness, love, and desire settled in them.

"What? What did you say?" He crossed the kitchen island and stood next to her, his hand caressing her arm.

"I said, I love you. And I want—"

He cut her words off by meshing his lips with hers. She sank into his body instantly, the hard planes of his muscles enfolding her.

Breaking off the kiss, his eyes softened as he looked at her. "Marry me."

Smiling, she exclaimed. "Yes. I want forever with you Cody."

His head tilted to one side as he crashed his lips to hers, the pancakes forgotten for now.

Acknowledgements

A big thank you to my editing team on this novel. My editor, Maddy Glenn from Softwood Self-Publishing and my proof-reader, Emily Morgans from Mischievous Ink.

Most of all, thank you for my readers. Thank you for picking up my book to entertain you. I would love to hear your thoughts on *Baby Be Mine*. Please leave a review on any review website. I greatly appreciate any words, even one or two sentences go a long way. The number of reviews a book receives greatly improves how well the book does. I'd love to hear from you too. I can be reached at www.chanellfaye.com.

Get the next book

To ensure you don't miss any Chanel L. Faye's next book, sign up to my mailing list: http://eepurl.com/hwqhgv

You can also follow me on social media to see any new updates:

<u>Bookbub</u>
https://www.bookbub.com/authors/chanel-l-faye

<u>Website</u>
www.chanellfaye.com

<u>Facebook</u>
www.facebook.com/chanellfaye72

<u>Twitter</u>
www.twitter.com/chanel__faye

<u>Instagram</u>
www.instagram.com/chanellfaye72